WITH LOTS OF LOVE AT CHRISTMAS
A Collection of Christmas Stories

LITTLE TIGER PRESS
An imprint of Magi Publications
1 The Coda Centre, 189 Munster Road,
London SW6 6AW
www.littletigerpress.com

First published in Great Britain 2010
This volume copyright © Magi Publications 2010
Cover illustration copyright © Alison Edgson 2010

THE SNOW ANGEL
Christine Leeson
Illustrated by Jane Chapman
First published in Great Britain 2006
by Little Tiger Press,
an imprint of Magi Publications
Text copyright © Christine Leeson 2006
Illustrations copyright © Jane Chapman 2006

THE CHRISTMAS BEAR
Anne Mangan
Illustrated by Joanne Moss
First published in Great Britain 1999
by Little Tiger Press,
an imprint of Magi Publications
Text copyright © Anne Mangan 1999
Illustrations copyright © Joanne Moss 1999

A CHRISTMAS WISH
Julia Hubery
Illustrated by Sophy Williams
First published in Great Britain 2007
by Little Tiger Press,
an imprint of Magi Publications
Text copyright © Julia Hubery 2007
Illustrations copyright © Sophy Williams 2007

HURRY, SANTA!
Julie Sykes
Illustrated by Tim Warnes
First published in Great Britain 1998
by Little Tiger Press,
an imprint of Magi Publications
Text copyright © Julie Sykes 1998
Illustrations copyright © Tim Warnes 1998

With Lots of LOVE at CHRISTMAS

A Collection of Christmas Stories

LITTLE TIGER PRESS
London

Contents

The Snow Angel

Christine Leeson   Jane Chapman

It was a bright, crisp morning when a swirl of wind woke Daisy mouse in the nest.

"Mum! Sam! Wake up," she squeaked excitedly. "It's Christmas! And it's been snowing!"

"Yippee!" yelled Daisy's brother Sam, dancing round the nest. "Happy Christmas, everyone."

"Happy Christmas, little ones," smiled Mum,
giving them each a parcel.

Daisy ripped off the wrapping. "Oooh!"
she squealed. "Berries!"

"And hazelnuts!" said Sam. "Thanks, Mum!"

Saving their presents for later, the mice rushed out to play in the snow.

"Have fun!" Mum called. "I'll find some extra bedding to make our nest cosy and later we can have a special Christmas tea."

Giggling, Daisy and Sam slipped and slid up the hillside. Below them the world sparkled under a blanket of snow but Daisy and Sam hardly noticed. High above their heads was the most beautiful thing they had ever seen. Sunshine gleamed on its wings as it soared through the sky.

"Sam, look," whispered Daisy. "It's an angel! A Christmas angel!"

But as the mice watched
breathlessly the angel
began to flutter and fall.
   "Oh no!" cried Daisy,
starting forwards as it
tumbled to the ground.
   "Quick!" Sam gasped.

With whiskers trembling
the mice tiptoed over
the snow.

The angel was lying silent and still. Its feathers shone like ice, and snow crystals glittered on its wings.

"Oh Sam!" Daisy cried. "Isn't it wonderful!"

"I don't think it looks very well," Sam replied anxiously.

At that moment, the snowy angel spoke.

"Little mice, can you help me?" it said. "My friends and I have flown for days, from a land of ice and stars, but last night I lost them in a storm. Now I am so tired and hungry and I don't know if I will ever see them again."

"Oh dear! We need to find food," said Daisy, "but everything is frozen."

"Not everything!" said
Sam. "Come on!"
And the mice raced
off across the meadow.

The snow was getting deeper as the mice returned, carrying their precious parcels of berries and nuts. They lay them in front of the lost and lonely angel and watched as, slowly, it began to eat.

Daisy brushed snowflakes from the angel's wings.

"Do you think it will be all right?" she asked as it lay its head down to sleep.

"I hope so," whispered Sam.

They waited by the angel's side until
at last the snow stopped falling and
sunset streaked the sky. Then the
angel opened its eyes.

With a sudden rush of feathers
it spread its wings.
  "Thank you, little mice," it said.
"You have been very kind. I will
  never forget your help."

The mice gasped as the angel soared up, over their heads, shining with gold in the evening light.

"Happy Christmas!" it called.

"Wow!" whispered Sam.

Daisy held up her paws.
"Look!" she cried. "It's
snowing again!"
   White flakes whirled
around them, but as Sam
reached out and caught
one he laughed in surprise.
"Feathers!" he shouted.

Quickly the mice
gathered armfuls of
soft, white feathers
and raced back home.

"Mum!" called Daisy. "We found an angel! It gave us a present!"

Mum looked up from the straw she'd been using to line their nest.

"Goose feathers!" she sighed. "We'll feel as if we're sleeping in the clouds tonight!"

Over Christmas supper Daisy and Sam
told their mum all about their beautiful
angel. Then, happy and tired, the family
snuggled up in a warm drift of feathers.

"That was the best Christmas ever!"
Daisy whispered to Sam. "We did see
a real angel, didn't we?"

"I'm sure we did," smiled Sam.

And, as he drifted off to sleep, he saw
the feathers shining in the darkness,
glittering like stars in a frosty winter sky.

The CHRISTMAS BEAR

Anne Mangan

Joanne Moss

It was nearly Christmas and it was snowing.
Inside the shop, among all the other toys, a little
bear was delighted. He was a polar bear and loved
snow.

Now that it was Christmas he hoped that he would
get a home at last. He had been waiting for a long
time. He was sure that someone would spot him in
the window and want a bear to match the Christmas
snow, but he was passed by every time.

"Someone must want me," thought the little bear gleefully, when he felt someone lift him from the window – until he heard her mutter, "That bear won't sell. He's taking up good window space."

The little bear was put on a high shelf inside the shop, to make room for a cute pink teddy. He sat there between a yellow monkey and a big doll.

"The longer you are in the shop the higher you go,"
whispered the monkey. "We're all forgotten now.
Children look on the lower shelves."

"Why wasn't I sold?" asked the little polar bear.

"Wrong shape and colour," said the monkey. "You look rather like a teddy bear, but you're not one. I've not been sold because I'm too yellow."

"And I'm too expensive," said the big doll.

"Cheer up! We can see lots of things from here."

The shop looked very cheerful with all the Christmas decorations, but a shop wasn't like a home, thought the little bear. He began to feel quite dizzy.

"I know! I've just
thought of something,"
said the monkey – and
he wriggled off the shelf,
right into a child's arms!

"You could do that," the doll told
the little polar bear.
"I'd be too afraid," he said.
"I daren't either," said the
doll. "I would break."
So the big beautiful doll
and the little polar bear
sat side by side and
waited and hoped . . .

A week before Christmas a lady and a little boy
came into the shop to buy a present for his sister.

"Becky already has lots of dolls," he said. "I want
something different."

The little polar bear's heart lifted. He certainly
was different. The assistant reached up and
took him down off the high shelf.

"He looks like a mistake," said the lady rudely.
"People will think we got him cheap."
They chose a calculator instead.

The little bear felt his insides sagging.
It was awful to be a mistake.

He flopped right over, and
someone picked him up,
gave him a shake,
and set him back
in his place.

The next day a girl came into the shop. She wanted a pretty toy to sit in her room and look nice. She saw the doll on the high shelf. "Exactly what I've been looking for," she cried. The big doll was overjoyed. She didn't want to be hugged and loved as the little polar bear did. She just wanted to look pretty.

The little polar bear missed the big doll dreadfully. He sat on his high shelf all alone, while people came in and out of the shop in a last minute rush to buy their presents for Christmas.

He saw so many toys being sold, and he wanted a home more than ever. If only someone would choose him!

It seemed as though the little polar bear's wish was granted, for suddenly someone looked up at him and said, "What a jolly little bear. I'll have him for my youngest. It's her birthday today."

The little polar bear was delighted. He didn't mind being bumped along in a bag, all the way to his new home.

"I've a lovely surprise for you!" the lady told her small girl. "Look!"

"Ugh!" said the child. "I don't want a silly bear. I wanted a racing car, you know I did." She threw the little bear across the room. Her mother picked him up again. "All right, darling. I'll change him for a car, shall I?"

The little polar bear was bumped all the way back to the shop, and put back up on the high shelf once more.

He felt worse than ever.

He had given up all hope of ever being wanted and loved.

On Christmas Eve a man and a woman with cheerful faces came into the shop.

"We'd like to buy a Christmas present for our niece," said the woman.

"A doll?" asked the assistant.

"Well, I don't know if she likes dolls," said the man. "Some do and some don't."

The man was so tall that he could see the high shelf easily. He noticed the little polar bear at once.

"How about this little fellow, Nicola?" said the man, taking down the little polar bear at once. "He's nice and soft. And snow-white like the North Pole."

"Yes, I think Elly will like him, Nicholas. Do let's buy him."

The little polar bear felt happy and afraid, all at the same time. "Suppose Elly doesn't like me?" he thought. "Suppose she thinks I'm a mistake? Suppose she wants a racing car instead?" He worried and worried as he was wrapped up in a Christmas parcel for the next day.

On Christmas morning, Uncle Nicholas and Aunt Nicola arrived at Elly's home. "We have an extra special present for you, Elly," said Uncle Nicholas.

Elly felt the parcel. It was very soft, like something she wanted to hug.

Then she opened it. Elly looked at the little bear and the little bear looked at Elly. "Do you like him?" asked Aunt Nicola.

Elly picked up the little bear and hugged him.
She buried her face in his soft fur.
"Oh yes," she cried. "He's the nicest present
I've ever had. I'll call him Nicky, after you both."
Elly took Nicky outside to let him see the snow.
Now the little polar bear had a home and a
name and someone to give him lots and
lots of hugs. He was the happiest
little bear in the world!

A Christmas Wish

JULIA HUBERY   SOPHY WILLIAMS

Gemma gazed up at the Christmas
tree. She'd watched excitedly as
Mum and Dad stood it up. She'd
cut the net, freed the branches . . .
and breathed in the magical
smell of Christmas.

At last it was time to unpack the decorations. Gemma's brother Ty danced round her knees impatiently. "Ty, calm down or you'll POP!" she laughed.

Gemma had told him all about the shiny baubles, the glittering tinsel . . . and her favourite, the leaping snow deer, who sparkled like ice and sugar.

One by one – oh so carefully – Gemma unwrapped the decorations.

At last she found the dusty box where
the snow deer slept. Ty spotted something
sparkly in the box, and reached out for it.
"Careful, Ty! Don't touch!" cried Gemma,
yanking the box away quickly – too quickly.
The snow deer fell from his hands . . .

There was the tiniest snap as
it hit the floor, and lay broken.
Now Gemma had no heart for
decorating the tree. Suddenly,
she hated Ty.

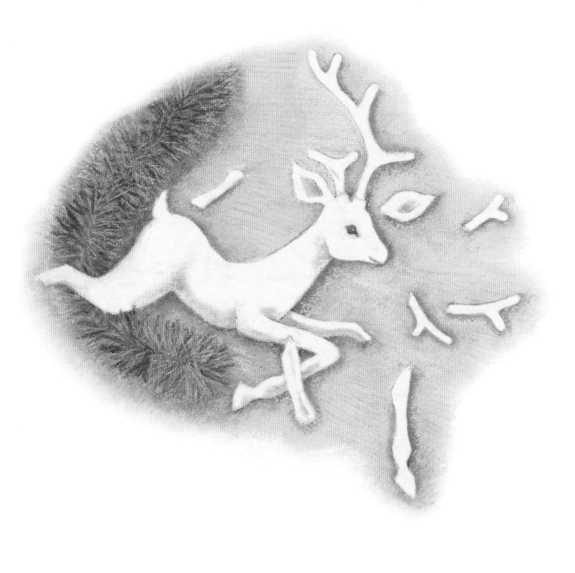

"Is something broken?" asked Mum.

"It's the snow deer, the one I really love, my snow deer. Stupid Ty broke him to bits," replied Gemma.

"It was an accident, Gem. You know how excited he is," said Mum.

Ty tried to say sorry. He brought
his favourite teddy to Gemma.
"Your teddy, Gemmie," he said.
Gemma wouldn't look at Ty.
She threw his teddy to the floor
and stomped out of the room.

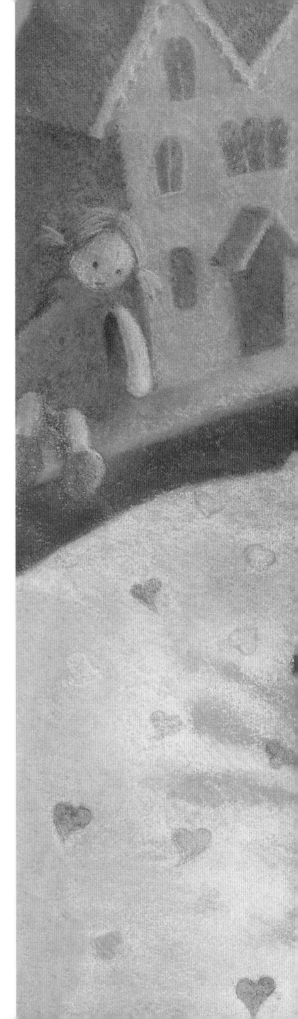

Gemma laid the snow deer on her pillow.
She remembered last Christmas: dark evenings,
sitting by the tree, dreaming with the snow deer . . .

... dreams where he carried her
through sparkling skies, high above
sleepy toy-town cities and patchwork
fields ...

. . . then higher still, riding a wild snowstorm
to the ice palaces of the North Pole. In crystal
halls shimmering with the light of a thousand
fairies they danced to a blaze of star-music,
spinning and whirling till the stars fell asleep,
one by one.

"Ty would have loved flying with the snow deer," thought Gemma. She remembered last Christmas Eve. Ty had bounced into her room in the middle of the night, because he wanted to see Santa's reindeer.

Then he had snuggled up with Gemma
like a big teddy bear.

"But he's better than a teddy – he hugs you
back!" thought Gemma. She began to feel
she'd been mean to Ty.

Gemma wondered how late it was. It was very quiet. She opened the door, and nearly fell over something. On the floor was a badly-wrapped parcel, and a little card with a big wobbly "sorry".

It was a pot of glue.
"To mend the snow deer!"
Gemma laughed.

Gemma crept downstairs.

"Look what Ty gave me," she whispered.

Working patiently, Mum and Gemma

stuck the snow deer back together.

"Now, it really is bedtime," said Mum.
But Gemma had one more thing to do.
She took the snow deer into Ty's room . . .

"Ty," she whispered, and the snow deer
flew down to brush his cheek with a kiss.
"He's better now," said Gemma. "Let's make a
Christmas wish. Maybe, just maybe, he'll fly
us to the stars."

Moonbeams kissed their sleepy heads as they
closed their eyes tight and wished . . .

. . . and together they flew high
above the sleepy towns into
the magical, velvet night.

Hurry, Santa!

by Julie Sykes

illustrated by Tim Warnes

It was Christmas Eve, and Santa's busiest
time of year.

"ZZZzzz," he snored from under his duvet.

"Wake up!" squeaked Santa's little mouse,
tugging at his beard. "Hurry, Santa! You
mustn't be late tonight."

"Ouch!" cried Santa, sitting up and rubbing
his chin. "Goodness, is that the time?
My alarm clock didn't go off and
I've overslept."

Santa leapt out of bed and began to pull
on his clothes. He was in such a hurry that
he put both feet down one trouser leg and
fell flat on his face.

"Hurry, Santa!" mieowed his cat. "You mustn't be late tonight."

"No, I mustn't," agreed Santa, struggling up. "I mustn't be late delivering the presents."

When he was dressed Santa hurried outside to his
sleigh. He picked up the harness and tried to put
it on the reindeer.

But the reindeer weren't there!

"Oh no!" cried Santa. "Wherever have they gone?"

"The reindeer are loose in the woods. You'd better catch them before they wander off," called Fox. "Hurry, Santa, you mustn't be late tonight."

"No, I mustn't," agreed Santa, running towards the trees.

Deep in the woods the reindeer
were having a snowball fight.
"Aaaaah!" cried Santa loudly,
as a snowball hit him in the face.

"Hurry, Santa," hooted Owl. "You haven't got time to play in the snow. You mustn't be late tonight."

"I wasn't playing!" said Santa indignantly. "Come on, you naughty reindeer, we've got work to do."

At last Santa was ready to leave. With a crack of his whip and a jingle of bells he steered the sleigh towards the moon.

"Go, Reindeer, go!" he shouted. "We mustn't be late tonight."

Around the world they flew, delivering presents to every child.

"Down again," called Santa, turning the sleigh towards a farm.

"Hurry, Santa!" answered the reindeer. "We're miles from anywhere, and the night's nearly over."

"I'm doing my best," said Santa, flicking the reins.

Before Santa could stop them the reindeer
quickened their pace.

"Whoa," Santa cried, but it was too late.
Landing with a bump, the sleigh skidded
crazily across the snow.

"Ooooh deeeaaar!" cried Santa in alarm.

CRASH!
The sleigh came to rest in a ditch.
Santa scrambled to his feet and rubbed
his bruised bottom. "Nothing broken,"
he boomed. "But we must hurry!"

When the reindeer had untangled themselves
everyone tried to dig out the sleigh. They tugged
and they pulled and they pushed as hard as they
could, but it was completely stuck.

"It's no good," wailed the reindeer. "We can't move this sleigh on our own."

"We must keep trying," said Santa. "The sky is getting lighter and we're running out of time."

Just then a loud neigh made Santa jump in surprise.
Trotting towards him was a very large horse.
  "Hurry, Santa!" she neighed. "You've still not
finished your rounds. *I'll* help you move your sleigh."
Everyone pulled together, even Santa's little mouse,
but it was no good. The sleigh was still stuck.

"Hurry, Santa!" called the cockerel from the gate.
"You must be quick. It's nearly morning."

"I am *trying* to hurry," puffed Santa. "I must deliver
the last of the presents on time."

Then suddenly the sleigh began to move . . .

. . . and Santa shot backwards,
cheering loudly.
"Hurry, Santa!" called all the animals.
"The sun's rising. You must be on your
way before the children wake up."

"Yes, I must," agreed Santa. "It's nearly Christmas Day!"

It was a close thing, but by dawn Santa
had managed to deliver every present.
"We did it!" yawned Santa. "I wasn't . . ."

Santa stopped talking and stared at his sack in dismay. At the very bottom there was still one present left. "Oh no, how awful!" he cried. "I've forgotten someone!"

Then Santa noticed that the animals were laughing.

"That present is for *you*. It's from all of us," said the reindeer.

"Hurry, Santa!" added Santa's little mouse.
"You must open your present. It's Christmas Day!"
"Yes, I must," chuckled Santa. "Now, I wonder what it is . . ."